Lily's Cat Mask

by Julie
Fortenberry

VIKING

For Annie, Kim, and my
North Carolina writing friends.

VIKING
An imprint of Penguin Random House LLC
375 Hudson Street
New York, New York 10014

First published in the United States of America by Viking,
an imprint of Penguin Random House LLC, 2017

LIBRARY OF CONGRESS CATALOGING-IN-PUBLICATION DATA IS AVAILABLE
ISBN: 9780425287996

Book design by Mariam Quraishi   Manufactured in China

1 3 5 7 9 10 8 6 4 2

Lily wasn't sure she wanted to get new things
for school, but her father said it would be fun.

When she got tired,
Lily just wanted to go home.

Then she saw the cat mask.

It was one-of-a-kind.
And her dad did something unusual.
He said "yes," and bought it for her.

She didn't need a shopping bag.
She wore it right out of the store.

Everywhere she went she wore the mask.
She wore it to parties with her closest friends.

She wore it to big family get-togethers
when she wanted to be invisible.

And when she wanted to be noticed.

She even wore it to the doctor.

Meow?

One day, she couldn't find the mask.

When her dad saw she was sad,
he made her a new one-of-a-kind
disguise.

It was fun to be a bunny for a while,
but she felt lucky to find the mask
a couple of days later.

She was so happy to be a cat
again, especially when she didn't
feel like talking.

She liked to hide her face when
she felt mean and couldn't get nice.

And she also made a very
important wish wearing her mask.

But when Lily started school, her teacher called the mask a distraction, and Lily was only allowed to wear it at recess.

Sometimes, she left the mask on,
hoping that no one would notice.

Sometimes the mask had to stay
in the teacher's desk drawer.

Then one day the teacher announced that at the end of the week they'd have a party—a costume party—and everyone could wear whatever they wanted!

There was a superhero, a mouse, a pirate,
a witch, a princess, a ghost, two bugs,
an alligator, and the very best one of all . . .

Another cat!